Jackson, 8 and Allegra, 5 live witl
and Dad in Connecticut. They hav
imaginations. Jackson is very good to Allegra
despite the occasional tease. Allegra is no
longer afraid of monsters.

Her father, Peter DaPuzzo had very little to do
with the writing of this book. It was almost
entirely written based on a game Allegra played
in her bedroom before going to sleep at night.

This book is dedicated to
those with wild imaginations.
Remember, it's up to you
what you believe in or not!

ISBN 978-0-9843477-3-5

Library of Congress number: 2011938502
Books-children illustrated

DaPuzzo, Peter. Author.
Gauvin, Matthew. Illustrator.
Foster-Fell, Jera. Digital file preparation, graphic design and layout.

Summary:
Allegra, a little girl, meets a fuzzy green monster who teaches her the importance of not judging a person by the color of their skin (or fur!)

Published by Web Profile Inc. Wolcott, Vermont.

Printed in the USA by Lightning Source.

Allegra

Friend of All

MONSTERS

By Allegra, Jackson and Peter DaPuzzo
Illustrated by Matthew Gauvin

Web Profile Inc, Publisher
Wolcott, Vermont

"...And the princess lived happily ever after",
says Mommy as she closes the book.

"No scary monsters came and ate her up?",
Asks a little frightened Allegra.

Mommy hugs her little girl tight and says, "No
honey, of course not. There are no such thing as
scary monsters. "

"But Jackson told me they come out at nighttime", Allegra says.

Mommy pulls the covers up tight and says, "That's only your big brother playing tricks on you. Monsters aren't real, they're only part of your imagination, so you shouldn't be afraid."

Mommy turns down the light and kisses her on the head. "Night, Night Sweetie."

"Night, Night Mommy", Allegra says trying to be brave.

Allegra closes her eyes and hears the wind blowing branches outside of her window. When she opens her eyes she sees a shadow of her teddy bear and is very afraid. She closes her eyes again and takes five deep breaths and finally drifts off to sleep.

When suddenly...

A short fuzzy green arm appears and taps on her shoulder.

"Umm hello, wake up!"

Allegra sits up startled.

"Hi there!", says a Fuzzy Green Monster, in a most friendly monster voice.

Allegra has to pick her head up to look over the edge of her bed because contrary to what she's been told, monsters aren't very tall.

Allegra wants to let out a cry, but after getting a good look at this ball of green fuzz standing on his tippy toes, she realizes she isn't really afraid, she's actually confused.

"Are you a mon, mon, mon?"

"A Monster? I sure am. The name's Fuzzy Green Monster. Nice to meet ya."

"So you don't want to eat me up?",
Allegra asks.

Fuzzy Green Monster thinks for a
moment scratching his fuzzy
green chin with his fuzzy green
finger and says, "Now that's a
funny question. Since when do
monsters eat people?"

Allegra says, "then what do monsters do?"

Fuzzy Green Monster replies, "Well... it's your imagination, it's entirely up to you."

Allegra swings her legs over the side of the bed and says, "So, you can be a Laughing Monster?"

"You bettcha", and he falls to the floor and laughs and rolls, and rolls and laughs in a very silly green fuzzy monstery sort of way.

"What about a Skipping Monster?"

"I can most certainly do that...
Why don't you join me?"

Allegra grabs her stuffed teddy bear
and starts skipping after the pint
sized ball of green fuzz...

Allegra stops skipping and asks, "What else can you do?"

"How about this..." And he turns his backside, wiggles his rump and sings. "Shake my booty, shake my booty now..."

Allegra laughs so hard she almost falls over.

"Now be a Jumping on the Bed Monster!" Allegra commands.

And they jump, and they jump, and they jump..

"Oh boy, If my brother could meet you. He'd be in for a big surprise. He told me that monsters EAT people when really there are no people eating monsters ..."

Allegra thinks for a moment.

"...there are only..."

"...TICKLE Monsters!", yells Allegra.

And Fuzzy Green Monster tickles her under her chin and she laughs, laughs, laughs as hard as she's ever laughed before.

Allegra says, "STOP Tickle Monster, stop! That tickles."

"Well, what did you expect?"

"Now be a Hugging Monster."

Fuzzy Green Monster wraps his little fuzzy green arms around her and gives her one giant fuzzy green monster HUG.

"Before I leave tonight, I want to become one more thing for you"

"What is that?" Allegra asks.

"Your friend."

"A Friend Monster?" asks Allegra.

"Yes, a Friend Monster", he says.

He digs in the toy chest and pulls out a wand and a gold crown. As he places the crown on her head he taps her on both shoulders with the wand and says, "Allegra, I pronounce you a Friend of All Monsters, tonight and forever, throughout the land."

Suddenly, the wind begins to swirl and the stars fall from the nighttime sky and swoop into the room.

Fuzzy Green Monster looks at Allegra and says, "Its time for me to go now my new friend."

With that, he grabs onto a swirling star, circles the room once and disappears into thin air...

Mommy walks into the room and opens the curtains. The sun is out and the birds are chirping.

Allegra opens her eyes and sits up in bed, confused.

"My, oh, my, miss sleepy head. You didn't make one peep last night! Did you have good dreams?" Mommy asks.

Allegra looks around her room and sees her teddy bear with the gold crown on its head and smiles.

"Yes Mommy. I had the best dreams ever."

CPSIA information can be obtained
at www.ICGtesting.com
Printed in the USA
253711LV00004B